GROSSET & DUNLAP
Published by the Penguin Group
Penguin Group (USA) Inc., 375 Hudson Street, New York, New York 10014, U.S.A.
Penguin Group (Canada), 10 Alcorn Avenue, Toronto, Ontario, Canada M4V 3B2
(a division of Pearson Penguin Canada Inc.)
Penguin Books Ltd, 80 Strand, London WC2R 0RL, England
Penguin Ireland, 25 St Stephen's Green, Dublin 2, Ireland
(a division of Penguin Books Ltd)
Penguin Group (Australia), 250 Camberwell Road, Camberwell, Victoria 3124, Australia
(a division of Pearson Australia Group Pty Ltd)
Penguin Books India Pvt Ltd, 11 Community Centre, Panchsheel Park, New Delhi - 110 017, India
Penguin Group (NZ), Cnr Airborne and Rosedale Roads, Albany, Auckland 1310, New Zealand
(a division of Pearson New Zealand Ltd)
Penguin Books (South Africa) (Pty) Ltd, 24 Sturdee Avenue, Rosebank, Johannesburg 2196, South Africa

Penguin Books Ltd, Registered Offices:
80 Strand, London WC2R 0RL, England

Angelina Ballerina © 2005 Helen Craig Ltd. and Katharine Holabird. The Angelina Ballerina name and character and the dancing Angelina logo are trademarks of HIT Entertainment PLC, Katharine Holabird and Helen Craig. Reg. U.S. Pat. & Tm. Off. Used under license by Penguin Young Readers Group. All rights reserved. Published by Grosset & Dunlap, a division of Penguin Young Readers Group, 345 Hudson Street, New York, New York 10014. GROSSET & DUNLAP is a trademark of Penguin Group (USA) Inc. Manufactured in China.

ISBN: 0-448-44134-9   10 9 8 7 6 5 4 3 2 1

This Scholastic edition published by arrangement with Penguin Group (USA) Inc.

Angelina Ballerina™

Angelina's Special Week

Grosset & Dunlap

Monday

Angelina Ballerina is a very busy little mouseling. On Monday afternoon, Angelina plays dress-up. She puts on a beautiful shawl and her mother's hat with big flowers on the brim. It's Angelina's favorite. When her mother comes home, Angelina says, "Look! I'm the fanciest mouseling in all of Chipping Cheddar!"

What makes your Mondays special?

Tuesday

On Tuesday, Angelina dances at Miss Lilly's
Ballet School. Angelina watches Miss Lilly and
has fun practicing all the steps with her. On
Saturday there will be a big performance and
Angelina wants to do her best.

What do you like to do on Tuesdays?

Wednesday

On Wednesday evening, Angelina helps her father in the kitchen. They pour and measure and mix everything into a great big bowl. Then they are ready to put dinner in the oven. What do you suppose they're making? Cheddar cheese puffs! Delicious!

Do you do something special on Wednesdays?

Thursday

On Thursday, it is bright and sunny. Angelina and her friend Alice ride their bikes up and down the bumpy roads. Angelina loves her birthday bicycle. When Alice shouts, "Come on, Angelina, let's have a race!" Angelina starts to ride faster and faster. "I'll beat you!" shouts Angelina.

What makes Thursdays special?

Friday

On Friday, Angelina and Alice ride all the way to Chipping Cheddar. At Mrs. Thimble's General Store, Angelina tells Mrs. Thimble she's doing errands for her mother. "My, but you are helpful!" says Mrs. Thimble. After Angelina gets everything on the list, she and Alice buy two big, beautiful balloons to tie on the handlebars of their bikes.

What is your favorite thing to do on Fridays?

Saturday

At last, it is Saturday night, the night of the performance. Angelina is the magic fairy in a real grown-up ballet. Her cousin Henry is a little elf. At the very end, Angelina does a perfect *jeté*, just the way Miss Lilly has taught her. Everyone claps and shouts, "Bravo!" Angelina has never felt so proud.

What do you like to do on Saturdays?

Sunday

Sunday is the most special day of all. Do you know why? Because on Sunday there is a BIG surprise waiting for Angelina at home… her new baby sister, Polly! Angelina holds the baby very carefully in her arms. She can't believe how delicate and little Polly is. "I'll be a good big sister," Angelina whispers softly.

What makes Sundays special?

What a busy week it has been for Angelina Ballerina. And just as one week ends, another one begins, full of more fun and surprises.

Wednesday	Thursday	Friday	Saturday	Sunday
	Morning	Morning	Morning	Morning
Afternoon	Afternoon	Afternoon	Afternoon	Afternoon

What a busy week it was!

Monday

Tuesday

Morning

Morning

Morning

Afternoon

Afternoon

Afternoon

Your days-of-the-week poster

Pull out the poster very carefully and hang it in a special place.

Use the stickers to mark the exciting things you're going to do each day.

When you write on the poster, use a pencil. It will erase easily so you can write over it next week.

Party time!

Party time!

Dance class

Dance class

Play date!

Play date!

Great day!

I drew a picture

Great day!

I read a book

Don't forget to...

Don't forget to...

I helped somebody